Trading Today for a Better Tomorrow

Trading Today for a Better Tomorrow

by Donald H. Lacy II

ReadersMagnet, LLC

Trading Today for a Better Tomorrow
Copyright © 2022 by Donald H. Lacy II

Published in the United States of America
ISBN Paperback: 978-1-957312-05-7
ISBN eBook: 978-1-957312-04-0

All rights reserved. No part of this publication may be reproduced, stored in a retrieval system or transmitted in any way by any means, electronic, mechanical, photocopy, recording or otherwise without the prior permission of the author except as provided by USA copyright law.

The opinions expressed by the author are not necessarily those of ReadersMagnet, LLC.

ReadersMagnet, LLC
10620 Treena Street, Suite 230 | San Diego, California, 92131 USA
1.619.354.2643 | www.readersmagnet.com

Book design copyright © 2022 by ReadersMagnet, LLC. All rights reserved.
Cover design by Ericka Obando
Interior design by Renalie Malinao

CONTENTS

Introduction vii

Understanding the Development of New Boundaries 1
The Opinion That Matters. 16
Negative Voices. 34
Creating The Attainable Goal 52
New Beginnings 69

INTRODUCTION

Many times in life we find ourselves seeking solace by the words of others who seem to be going through the same struggles as we are. Through them we never seem to find the inspiration to get out of the rut we're in and cannot seem to understand why.

Inspiration is only useful when it comes from a source that has already conquered the trial we are currently going through because that source has found the path to the resolution. In today's world of personal or financial struggles, whether it is for women or men, child or adult, we need the voice of one who has already found peace in his or her own mind. Each case and life struggle is different in application but not in context. Inspirational words require action; therefore the words are nothing more than a starting point for recovery. They include a point of view describing the situation and a direction for life restoration.

Throughout the course of this book, a foundation for the most basic struggles is defined and a path for mental recovery is established. All quotes are original and are inspired through real-life application.

Through the years, not only have I found ways to mentally overcome my shortcomings, but through watching others I have also been able to help them find their path as well. Early in my adult life I struggled with getting angry when someone made a negative comment about me. I would just either lash out or simply give up instead of learn from what they said and make life adjustments. Because of this I became very introverted and therefore lonely. I never carried a great deal of confidence in anything I attempted until I actually saw positive results. I allowed others to direct me away from my dreams and into the same life others were leading, which was accepting what was present in my life and not reaching for more.

I then started reading autobiographies and studying the lives of those who had reached higher planes in life. I realized that regardless of what anyone said or thought of them, they never strayed away from their goals and dreams. Instead, they used the negative feedback as the driving force behind what they desired to accomplish. Once I realized that they learned from every failed endeavor and changed how they addressed those situations, I realized I could do the same thing.

Even today I encourage my children to read and then talk to them about what the characters had to overcome so they can see that even in fiction, goals must be met to accomplish anything. Reading and looking for understanding of what was read is changing their young lives, just as it has changed my life.

Over many years I have found a peace that I never thought possible when I was twenty years old or even thirty, but I eventually found that peace and continue to educate myself and grow. Today, even in the most trying moments, I am able to calmly find a resolution because I know that the only thing I can control in my life is me and I have accepted that everything else around me can and will change. If I manage my own mind, then everything I encounter in life will eventually have the resolution I desire. I always accept those ventures that have an end result separate from what I desire as an education for a better tomorrow. I will learn what does not work, and eventually, through education and trial and error, I will get that result that I am seeking.

I pray that the words I share with you in this book inspire all who read it to find the same inner peace that I have found and have been able to share with many others.

UNDERSTANDING THE DEVELOPMENT OF NEW BOUNDARIES

Beginning in the early stages of our lives, we are trained to believe that we are limited in what we can ultimately accomplish over that lifespan. This is taught to us by the tests we take in school, words from parents who tell children they are failures and won't accomplish anything in life, and the words of our peers. It is fed to us so often that eventually we start to believe in it. Once we believe the things others say about us, we no longer aspire to be anything but what we have been coached to become. These words are defined as the negative influences in our lives.

This negative attitude has created a society of individuals who are only able to accomplish a fraction of what they should be able to accomplish in life. Then we collectively lay back and look at the two percent of our society that are deemed successful and say things like, "I wish I would have thought of that," or "I could have done that too." That two percent of society is in actuality the two percent of people who were willing to venture beyond what people said they could accomplish and reached beyond the thoughts and words of others to prove that nothing is unattainable if you have the right drive and education.

> One's success is only limited by what is perceived attainable in the mind and by the effort one is willing to put forth to attain that goal.

If you don't believe you can accomplish something, then the reality is that you can't. Once you've developed the thought that something is beyond your grasp, then you are no longer capable of putting forth the necessary effort to accomplish that feat. Just because the business model Bill Gates created for Microsoft was not considered a great idea at the time does not mean the business idea would not become a successful business venture. He dreamed beyond what people thought was possible and believed he could accomplish it. Even if he had fallen short of his desired outcome, because he reached beyond his dream, the accomplishment was still great. Once the initial goal was reached he set new standards for himself and has now reached even beyond what he had probably imagined.

So ask yourself this question: How can I train myself to reach for new goals knowing that I have been trained in the past to not see beyond the limits created by others? The key here is that the limits were created by others and are now harbored as fears in our minds of reaching beyond their perceptions of what our true ability is. When you took aptitude tests in school, they were to tell you, based on a score, what you should or could aspire to be in life. And the results varied from feeding the animals at the zoo to working for NASA. As you reflect back over your life, how many people who were supposed to accomplish great things throughout their lives were actually able to do so? What about those individuals that society deemed limited in their ability? Some are judges and CEOs of large corporations. What makes them any different that you and me?

My challenge to you at this point is to create value within yourself. Do you have mental strength and stability beyond that of an animal? Although it may seem you do have it today, I have a test for you to verify this stability that you believe you have in your mind. How far beyond your normal daily rituals do you venture? What was the last goal you set that was accomplished, and when did you set a new one? This is important to identify where you are regarding your mental strength and your drive.

Small animals in all species begin by clinging to the mother. Every few days they venture a little farther from the mother to view other parts of their living area. Over time, they are able to venture anywhere they desire. This is possible because each day that they venture into new territory, it expands their world and breaks down the barriers set the previous day. Over the next few days, that new area becomes part of the norm for them and allows them to expand even farther the next time they venture out into the world because what is new today is normal tomorrow.

> Once you see beyond others' perceptions of what you can't do, you will find that it is limitless what you can do.

Using real-life applications are always the best way for us to see how limitless our abilities can reach when we desire to reach beyond what others see as limitations for us. Although examples appear general, we can always look to general associations to find real life applications. Think back to the people you went to high school with. Now think of the person you thought wasn't very smart or was quiet and an afterthought in the minds of most people. Today, when you look at that person, you may see that he is working for the local government, running his own business, or something beyond the scope of what anyone ever thought possible for him. Why did this person aspire to such heights? The answer is simple. He set goals above what was expected of him because he believed there were no limitations to what he could accomplish.

> Success is not measured by the goal, but by the effort required to attain it. Each accomplished goal is always followed by a new goal, but we reflect on the journey more often than we do the accomplishment in order to find the value.

Whenever you accomplish something new in life, there is a tendency to talk about what you went through to accomplish that feat. We are always happy to find success in something we aspired to do, but we take pride in the effort we were willing to put forth to accomplish it. Sadly, people tend to limit themselves to the small things and never aspire to be anything beyond that. Today is a new day. So let's become that small animal and look to venture beyond where we are today so that tomorrow our world has expanded. It can be personal, business, or relational. But creating small goals and reaching for them will take us beyond where we are today and expand what is the norm for tomorrow.

Ultimately, a goal is nothing more than creating an avenue that takes a restriction on what we are today, limits we placed on ourselves mentally, and removing that barrier to make it a reality. Keep in mind that a flaw is nothing more than the perception that something that is natural to us is abnormal in the eyes of others. The important thing here is that it is nothing more than a perception or someone else's opinion. So what is a dream today needs to become reality tomorrow.

What in your life would you like to change first? Is it a relationship that is not going according to how you would desire for it to go? Is it a dream that you may have discounted as impossible because you lack the necessary knowledge to accomplish the dream at this time? The first step in changing the way we think about ourselves is simple, even though it may seem difficult. Identify our shortcomings, because we can't be responsible for others' shortcomings or areas they desire to improve within themselves.

Step one, as I said, is simple. Life is situational, not personal. Look at the things in your life that you normally become highly emotional over and think about the reaction you have because of it, whether it is a word someone says to you or an action by someone else that goes against your own principles. It could be something at work or, if you're a parent, something at school that affected your child. You will have an emotional response to a situation that affects decision making. It is just a situation and can be addressed and resolved without affecting the outcome of an entire day emotionally. Things that are personal linger and can change how you approach life on a daily basis, whereas situations only last for the moment and then are no longer a part of your emotional state. Once you deal with a situation, you no longer have to worry about it, because you can't change the fact that it has already occurred. It simply teaches you a lesson so you know how to handle the same or similar situation in the future and therefore, should be counted as educational. So why not confront the issue when it happens, so it does not affect anything beyond that moment. Allowing it to linger allows it to affect your thinking, as well as your emotional state, over a period of time, thus making it personal. The number three cause of divorce when women are polled is lack of communication from men, according to *Lifestyle* writer Linda McCloud. The problem with that is that it has to be communication between two people, not one. The number-one reason for infidelity is also the lack of communication with couples, according to In fidelity-etc.com. People are seeking something that they feel is missing in life or in the relationship. What is the main statement behind the action? "I just needed someone to talk to because the person I'm with doesn't talk to me anymore." Again, it's a situation that could have been avoided or resolved by just dealing with it instead of making it personal and not addressing it when it first became an issue. Had the person talked about it when the feelings were there initially, the situation could have changed or been avoided.

Over the course of a month, I talked with a gentleman who stated he had issues with his temper when dealing with the woman in his life. He stated that whenever he arrived home and the house was not clean, he would confront his spouse and an argument would ensue. On occasions, she would leave because these seemed unbearable to her. So I talked to him about changing the situation, which required changing how he approached it. Again, real-life applications have a tendency to drive points home. So we created a short game plan to change the situation and remove the personal perceptions that were created in his mind. He needed to reprogram himself into seeing that he could manipulate a situation where he could not manipulate personal emotions. He needed to venture somewhere mentally that he had never envisioned himself venturing before.

So what did he have to do to change this? He had to go home and see things as out of order; manage the situation by making it "us" instead of "me." The next time he arrived home and things seemed in his eyes to be in disarray, he walked in and immediately kissed his spouse and son, changed clothes, and started picking up a room and asked if she would help him. Now the perception is changed because she doesn't feel she's doing it alone. The situation is also changed, because now he has made himself a part of the resolution.

> When we seek a resolution to a problem, we cannot expect our desired results if we're leaving the effort to resolve the issue in the hands of others.

You can't manage a problem if you're not a part of the resolution. Once the house was clean and it became a regular pattern, it no longer was an unmanageable situation because it became a part of his regular routine. At this point, he had expanded where he could venture in terms of the home and in terms of managing his own emotions. Now he was able to expand into a new area and create new avenues to evolve and grow the relationship. He found a way to make the resolution a part of his own daily routine.

Although there was much more involved in the growth, this is an example of dealing with and understanding your situation and managing or dealing with it by expanding your world and becoming a part of the solution.

The roadblocks are mental, and one must desire to change the situation before one can make a physical change to it.

> To overcome an obstacle, one must first recognize that there is an obstacle. The mind allows one to use one's own limitations and view them as flaws in others instead of realizing it is a fear in us that keeps us from recognizing the need for change in ourselves.

Now we understand that we need to start by expanding our boundaries and understanding that our limitations are established in our own minds. It is important to be realistic and remember we can only walk one step at a time. Once you establish the fact that you are able to take one step, you can then feel comfortable taking the second step. After each step has been taken, and through trial and error, you find that you are walking. But it must be done one step at a time; you can't practice step ten without first getting through steps one through nine. Starting with step ten gets you out of the routine of the first nine and ultimately renders you back to step one. You risk falling, or in the case of life, failing to complete a task successfully.

Sometimes the end result is step ten, but the resolution may have been in steps one through four or steps five and six, but how would you know without going through every step? Make every step the routine in managing your daily life, and you will find that the old situation doesn't return because you are following the steps you established to resolve it. Life is about expanding routines, not remaining in the same ones.

Keeping a personal journal with goals, the trials you have gone through, and the goals you are attempting to reach, as well as the victories you have enjoyed, is essential to this growth. This is easily the most important step for personal goals and establishing new boundaries if you're having trouble establishing them. Once they're on paper and you read them, it's a lot easier to verify that they are realistic. What the mind deems as realistic does not necessarily confirm that it is realistic. In your mind, you can establish that today you are a grocery store bagger but believe you have the qualities to be CEO of the company; but once you write it down, you can see where you are in life versus where you want to be, what you're going through, and what you want to accomplish or what the next step is in order to reach that ultimate goal. You view your current skills and what skills are necessary to handle the job function that you desire. Then you can determine if the thought was or is realistic, regardless of what area in your life you want to expand, not just in your career; it could be on the relational level as well. Write your goals down and keep them realistic in the scope of what you are actually able to accomplish in the short term. Then establish your long-term aspirations. Follow that with a game plan to reach each of them. If you need assistance, find a network of people who have already reached the place that you are reaching for to get an understanding of what was required to get there. Others who have already traveled the path can tell you what steps they followed to get to where they are, including the obstacles they needed to overcome.

> Personal success is found after one is able to manage one's situations and control one's emotions, remembering that negative emotions are direct results of situations becoming personal.

Once you understand how to manage situations, you will find that your reach is limitless; then you can begin to reach out beyond what you once perceived as unattainable. Clearly, no one is immune to the negative thoughts associated with success beyond what we can readily see. The difference between those who achieve and those who don't is in the drive to overcome the fear of failure. To overcome that fear, those who achieve simply had to capture the true understanding of what failure is. Failure is nothing more than not attaining one's reasonable goal through the lack of effort, education, or a willingness to pay the necessary price for that success.

Let's change our perspective on how we want to walk through life. Let's treat this phase as chapter one in the freedom from mental restrictions. The beginning of anything is completed over time, not in a few minutes or a few days. The learning curve is different for each person, but the end result can always be the same. We will create a starting point by creating some simple guidelines for ourselves. We will start with how we see ourselves and how we handle situations that arise in our lives.

The hardest thing for a person to do is to be honest with themselves about their own abilities. Either we are not giving ourselves enough credit for our ability, or we're giving too much credit to our limited ability. So for step one, we are changing our long-term goals into short-term goals until we have established the basics of managing our thoughts and developed the ability to overcome seeing challenges as restrictions. Today, I am able to run a mile comfortably, and after I reach the one-mile point, my legs are tired and I am fatigued. So each day I run that same mile, and when I reach the mile point, I run beyond it by one hundred meters. It may be difficult to complete the one hundred additional meters, but I push as close to it as I can each day. Each day it becomes a little easier to run that additional one hundred meters, until it becomes a part of my everyday routine. Once I've established that it is a part of my routine, I add another one hundred meters to the run. Eventually, if you desire, you will be able to run a marathon. It doesn't happen overnight, but over time. We create good habits that allow us to accomplish our ultimate goals in life.

If you aspire to be a manager at work, what would you do first? To begin, you must create good habits and expand your boundaries. You would start by becoming more social and organized in your everyday life so that it becomes routine. Establish yourself as the person others come to with questions, because you have developed a good sense about your current position and have become an authority. You would need to communicate well with everyone, not just the people close to you, so you start with your social circles. Each day, week, or month, you should attempt to meet someone new. Practice speaking with customers and coworkers in a professional manner and avoid using language that is not considered professional. Over time, the changes will no longer be something you practice but instead a part of your everyday routine and again, will have expanded your boundaries. It's a new boundary that you established and control. Once established, you can then move to the next phase, which is communicating with your manager. Verify what job functions and qualities are necessary to be successful at the job. I say communicate with your manager because they would be the best resource since they would have already reached where you aspire to go. You would then need to make those things a part of your everyday routine so when you do reach that goal, the things necessary for the venture to be successful are already things you do naturally.

With a new boundary established and the goal attained, you can now create the next goal and start by creating and expanding into the new boundaries to make the transition not only smooth but possible.

> The boundaries in life should be as limitless as the boundaries of our imagination.

Life is about trial and error. No one has ever reached the highest levels of success without failing to attain those goals in the beginning. They learned from them, made documentation, and began again from step one until they found the level of success in that endeavor to bring it to a completed state. What they did was change how they set up and managed their goals. Until you teach yourself to complete the small tasks, it is not necessary to create long-term aspirations. The reason they are called longterm goals is because they require a lot of work over time. If you aren't trained to complete the small tasks, then you will never finish the larger ones. The task required to reach the ultimate goal will always seem too difficult to overcome because you don't know how to manage your mind and dictate solutions through education. So when I say to only focus on the small goals, it is so you can establish a pattern of expanding those boundaries one step at a time. Once you establish those positive habits, then you can have bigger dreams, because you will have established a pattern of finishing whatever you start.

When a scientist begins an experiment, he follows it step by step. Through trial and error, he eventually reaches the conclusion he was seeking. In order to get there, regardless of where the error occurs, he always starts from the beginning, taking notes and establishing a pattern of consistency. This is how life can and should be approached. Every new venture in life is simply an experiment to expand our knowledge and abilities. Constant is you, and everything else is a variable, just like an experiment. You can only control what you are doing on a daily basis, not the actions of others.

Today is nothing more than yesterday's tomorrow. Since each day is a new day, make today and this moment more meaningful than yesterday and the last moment.

- I will include what positive things I learned yesterday and add them to my new adventures today.
- I will establish new boundaries in a limitless world, training myself to be better each moment and creating positive habits that will allow me to attain every goal I desire to attain.

- Time is only a factor in establishing the time of day, but not in the completion of the task at hand.
- Whatever the length of time required, I am trained to mentally accept it as necessary to reach my ultimate level of completion in any task I set forth to complete.

I would like to ensure that we have a clear understanding that establishing new boundaries is not an end, but a beginning. There is more required to becoming self-motivated and inspired. Becoming self-motivated is the first step of many to becoming what we desire to become. We will remove the barriers that established in us the thought that we are limited in what we can accomplish. We will establish the understanding that the only limits in life are those we harbor in our own minds. Next, we will eliminate the long-term, unrealistic goals we have in our minds and establish good habits of completing the simple tasks in life. Once we establish the right habits, what was once unrealistic is now realistic. We will follow up with writing down ideas and goals, along with a game plan for completing those tasks. This will also be a complement to creating good habits.

The only reason a goal can be deemed unrealistic is if we have not established the personal groundwork for completing such a task. Now it is time to organize our lives and begin expanding who and what we are as individuals. We are not remaking who we are, but instead expanding on a solid foundation and removing mental barriers created by established society. Understand that any limits that we have, even if given to us by others, are nothing more than barriers created in the mind. If we believe it is so, then it will be. If you don't believe you can accomplish great things, you won't; if you think you're not smart enough to do something, you're not. Not because you don't have the mental capacity to accomplish it, but because you've accepted as fact the idea that you lack the necessary tools to accomplish it. Once your mind has accepted something as fact, it is a fact until you are able to validate the contrary. But it is not because of others that you're not, but instead because of you and what your beliefs are in yourself. Break down the belief barriers that tell you that you are anything less than what you can be. See your own potential by expanding on who you are today, in spite of what was accomplished yesterday. And stop putting off tasks meant for today until tomorrow. The easiest thing in life to do is to say, "I'll do it tomorrow." Tomorrow is the never-ending excuse because it is the primary constant in life. Until the last breath of life, it is always an available escape from responsibility.

Excuses are always available to the person who does not desire to try. Excuses allow people to lay blame for their lack of drive or success at the feet of other sources. They blame time, parents blame the responsibility of being a parent, and spouses blame one another. The fact is the only person responsible for an adult's lack of drive and desire is the one who desires to accomplish the feat. Anything you can directly impact the outcome of is your own responsibility.

Eliminating excuses is just as important in expanding your new boundaries as education. Once you expand your mind to no longer make excuses for not putting forth the effort to do something, you will find that you complete more tasks because it is second nature in your life. You have established the positive habit of completion.

> Once you establish the right habits, it is easy to establish the building blocks necessary for a better tomorrow.

So how do we set the framework that establishes these new habits? We must first establish the areas where we feel inferior or weak. We all must understand that the flaws are nothing more than the opinion that something about us is either unnatural or not acceptable. In a world of ignorance, would not intelligence be considered a flaw? Accepting responsibility for our thoughts and ideas is the first step. We need to establish understanding that we have to depend on ourselves to establish the necessary framework for those positive habits in our lives.

THE OPINION THAT MATTERS

The older we become, the harder it is to break the cycle of not being able to change our way of thinking. We tend to get caught up in our own predictable patterns of life, so much so that we can't create a new cycle of change within ourselves. Our expectation is always the same. We accept the inability to change as something normal instead of a mental prison. We identify the areas in our lives that we need to improve upon and then never act on the changes we deem necessary for growth, not because we don't want to change, but because we don't know how to differentiate the person we are with the personality that imprisons us for growth and mental stability.

You can never change the core person if you don't free yourself from a mindset that your world is not expandable but instead limited on what is available to you. We do, on the other hand, have the ability to change the personality of that core person. Part of your personality is adjusted in developing and expanding the boundaries in which you are able to travel. This is both mentally and socially available, as we learned in "Understanding the

Development of New Boundaries." The rest comes from one's desire to be a better person mentally.

Let's start by revisiting a word we will be using a lot over the next few pages: *opinion*. The reason the word will be visited a lot is because it is the key to overcoming or surrendering to what restricts one's success. If one feels his physical appearance is a flaw, it is only because he accepted someone else's opinion about him as fact. It doesn't mean it is a fact, only that he has accepted it as so and therefore, in his mind, it is a fact. Thus his body language and facial expressions change when someone looks upon him, because of his insecurity about his own appearance. The same rules apply with someone who deems him or herself beautiful.

So how do we change the perceptions of ourselves in our minds? If all phases of growth are associated, then this will be nothing more than a new boundary that one is attempting to expand into. Just as the first chapter is about establishing new boundaries for growth in life, this is a new boundary necessary for mental development. Whenever we change anything about our lives, it is a new boundary. Every new phase we enter into during our lives, and every goal we achieve success in, is nothing more than an expansion of our boundaries. Whether it is social or mental, we are expanding over time to limitless levels.

> It is easier for one to accept the negative as truth than to accept the positive as fact.

The biggest weakness a person can have is in believing that he or she is not smart enough to successfully complete a task. Harboring such thoughts disables the ability to try anything that requires thought and hard work. Your mind has been trained to accept a negative opinion and an inaccurate thought. So how do we change this perception in ourselves?

Let's understand our basic makeup first; then we will expand into the mental cure. The first thing one must do is understand that accepting unsubstantiated opinions as fact is the true flaw. Flaws are simple to understand but difficult to overcome. The older a person is, the harder it is to overcome the restrictions that time has placed on us mentally. The important thing to remember when writing down goals is to be realistic about what we can accomplish today. Once we've established what we can do today, we can begin focusing on where we can go tomorrow.

The views of others affect the view we have of ourselves today but will not be the view we have of ourselves tomorrow. Just because someone feels you don't possess the skills to complete a task does not mean you don't possess them. It only means they have a low opinion of your skill set. They don't know the drive you have or the ability you have to solve the tasks necessary to successfully complete the requirements of dream fulfillment. Only you know what type of drive you have.

> My desire and drive to be more successful is fueled by a desire to prove the negative opinions of me wrong.

The way a person perceives others is a direct result of how that person perceives him or herself If you talk to a person with high self-esteem and high moral value, he or she has a tendency to lift you up to just short of the level where he or she is. No one can push you above 80 percent of what they are because the knowledge they can share does not exceed that potential. So when someone is degrading you or you think they are attempting to lower your opinion of yourself, take solace in that fact that they have to bring you to 80 percent of what they are. If they need to bring you down, then you're already ahead of them. Why travel in reverse when you destination is in front of you?

Although the opinions of others should not be important in terms of how you manage your life, it is important to know the opinions that others harbor about you. They are important because we need to be aware of what it is about us that drives our belief that we are limited in what we can accomplish. Is it the opinion of others today that drives that belief, or is it the opinions from our past that we have allowed to affect us? Either way, we need to take steps to change our way of thinking about ourselves.

It's time for a change, and the first step in that change is identifying who we allow to influence our decision making. Which statements made from your past dictates what you perceive as a truth about yourself? These things are necessary because before you can solve a problem, you must first identify and consider the source. Clearly, the source of such thought has been given power over us through influence.

Depending on how long you have been allowing others to influence you will determine how hard it will be to overcome the negative thoughts. The more important a role a person has played in one's life in regard to development, the more they will factor into how difficult it is to overcome the negative opinion of you that is harbored in your mind.

If you are close to your parents and they have ridiculed you for not successfully completing something, you may harbor a fear of failure into adulthood. You will not attempt anything that requires risk or trial and error. That fear was created by the influence of another and the desire to be socially accepted by them; thus you now carry a fear of failure, the belief that anything short of their expectations is a failure. Thus you established a weakness in your character.

Once identified, it becomes a stepping stone for your future success. The person, regardless of who is giving an opinion, has dictated through fear your decision making concerning your future. Their thoughts or words were nothing more than opinions that you allowed to dictate how you manage your own desires and drive. The problem is the words were nothing more than opinions shared over long periods of time that you allowed your mind to accept as factual. The thoughts were reinforced into your mind until you came to the conclusion that they were true.

Because you accepted those opinions as fact, others around you are able to read into your fears and are able to dictate additional barriers in your mind. Now you are able to be influenced academically and socially. Every shortcoming diminished your opinion of yourself, until you became the person you are today. You now find yourself only attempting those things that appear easy and within the scope of your everyday life. The barriers that were placed keep you from venturing beyond the established boundaries of comfort. You look at your dreams as unrealistic and question your ability mentally and physically to accomplish tasks beyond your current mental scope. You fear the individual reactions of those people if you are not able to successfully complete a task. Have you ever heard someone, or even yourself, use the excuse for not doing something, "I don't want my dad/mom to be disappointed in me"?

You can't develop new boundaries until you stop allowing the opinions of yesterday to influence the actions for today. Interestingly enough, you can't change tomorrow with the fears of today any more than you can change the weather. Words or thoughts without basis are nothing more than opinions. If the opinion that space was unreachable had been accepted, NASA would not exist today. Every technological advance began as an idea and became reality because someone believed in him or herself and an idea enough to understand the idea of trial and error would be overcome. With every great discovery there was someone or some group that would say it wasn't possible. But the reason those inventors succeeded in their quest was because they did not listen to those opinions. Each time they were not successful in their venture, they were a little closer to success because they had eliminated an obstacle. They started over, identified the things that went wrong, and corrected the error. They were educating themselves along the way and eventually found the success they originally planned for.

You may not be a scientist, but you have the same ability to change your own life. Is not your life the same as those experiments? Were you born walking, or did you crawl first? Did you crawl right away, or did you start by rolling over and learning how your legs influenced movement? How many babies start by moving forward? Very few babies start by going forward. In fact, the usual beginning is scooting backward. Through encouragement, we learn to scoot forward. Then we eventually began to crawl. Even though we fell, our parents and other family members kept encouraging us to stand up and take that first step. That first step became two then three. Eventually, we would fall no more and that walk became a run. In every case, we were able to expand where we could venture in our lives because our mind was encouraged and we continued to learn and develop. But that encouragement stopped as we got older, and the tasks exceeded those of the people who were encouraging us in the beginning.

We learned to count as well as how to read and write. How much different are our other dreams and goals than the ones we had from birth? They're more advanced because our minds are more advanced, but they are still part of the same process. Without that encouragement, we seem to believe we can't go forward. That encouragement, or lack of encouragement as we got older, became a tool of deceit in our minds. We actually believed we needed that encouragement to be successful. In fact, in many cases, we became dependent on those words of encouragement or discouragement to determine what we would or would not attempt in our lives. We used them as a safety net to keep us from overcoming the more difficult trials and to avoid risk.

Identify what it is you want to do with your life. Compare what you want to do with the reason you are not working toward it. If it is nothing more than you not believing you can accomplish it, then it will be attainable, as long as it is realistic, in the timeframe you have set to reach the goal and if you take the steps necessary to overcome the fear of failure.

Identifying the reason is usually harder than it appears. People tend to believe the things they are told by others instead of having faith in themselves and their own ability. Whether it was told by parents, peers, and teachers as a youth, love interests today, or peers at work, we tend to believe we cannot accomplish any more than we already have in our lives. This is as far from the truth as anything anyone will ever be able to say to you. You are limited by your mind, not by other people's words or actions.

Does the opinion of someone who has never accomplished any of their goals matter to someone reaching for their own goals? If someone has never overcome the struggle you're going through, then how can they coach you to overcome your trials or tell you that it can't be accomplished? Life, as stated previously, is about trial and error. We are all going to make mistakes or come up short at times. The idea is to learn from our shortcomings and establish new boundaries with the right information to keep us from repeating the errors we made along the way.

It doesn't matter what someone says to you, whether it is positive or negative. If they haven't overcome what you're going through, or are attempting to establish, then what they say can only be viewed as an opinion and nothing more. If the opinion is negative, then it should be fuel to prove them wrong. Either way, it should be viewed as a means of encouragement. In sports, negative comments are used as bulletin board material to inspire the team to play harder and prove those statements wrong. How is life any different in terms of encouragement? Look at the source of the comments or thoughts expressed to you. If the comments are regarding a business you dream of starting, ask yourself how long the person giving negative feedback has been running a successful business? If it's regarding something as simple as physical fitness, how developed is that person's body? There is not a single person who does not desire to be better at the majority of the things that are part of their everyday lives. The only thing that allows you to overcome those shortcomings is actually going out and doing something about it. You have to change your mental view of yourself today in order to change your direction tomorrow.

> Every walk must begin with a first step, and every first step begins with standing up. Be inspired to stand up so you may begin walking in a new direction.

I had a problem with depression. I would get down because I felt life wasn't treating me fairly. I looked at the success of others and listened to people tell me that what I wanted to do was not available to people like me because people from communities like I came from accomplished very little. So I decided to fall into that type of life as well. One day I realized I wanted to do better things with my life.

I always wanted to work with computers in some capacity when I lived in Michigan. Back in the nineties, if you didn't have a job with General Motors or one of the company's affiliate plants, you were considered second class almost. At least that's how I felt. I worked many jobs that were always considered second tier financially. I even found one at the truck plant where I spent time working for a subcontractor, so I finally decided to leave the plant and try something different.

First, I tried delivering food and working for a food distribution service. I moved to North Carolina, and financially, things got worse, but I never quit. I went to the library, looked up jobs in Arizona, and before I left I had a job in Tempe. There had been many struggles financially--I have been homeless twice-- but eventually I got a job with a software company where I spent almost seven years doing what I dreamed of doing. I educated myself on the different aspects of the business, and even today I continue to seek out more education in that field, even though I am no longer employed in it. The dream was fulfilled, and now I have moved on to another.

Financially I may not be where I want to be, but I will get there because I will never stop reaching for my goals and fulfilling my dreams. Once one endeavor has been fulfilled, it is time to move to the next one. I will keep learning, keep growing, and keep dreaming bigger tomorrow than I did today. I will always live by my own personal motto: You can't change yesterday, so live today in a way that leaves you no regrets tomorrow.

I realized on my own that the people who were discouraging me from doing better were stuck in the same rut as I was. I came to the conclusion that they couldn't tell me what it was like to travel if they had never left their own neighborhood.

So I made a plan for what I wanted to do first. I looked for a job in a different city and was actually interviewed over the phone. I then found an apartment there close to the job I had found. I put money together for the trip and for the apartment. The next thing was to map out the trip and locate places for gas and food along the way. Of course, like every plan, there are things that happened that could be discouraging. The car began overheating, and we found that the radiator had a leak and would not allow my pregnant wife, my children, and me to successfully make the trip. So that was money we hadn't planned for, but instead of being discouraged, we replaced the radiator in my mother's driveway, setting the trip back by a few hours, but refusing to be discouraged. Late that night, we packed up the family and my pregnant wife, along with the kids, and we made the trip to our new city.

Things weren't easy there. The job didn't work out, and we eventually ended up in a worse situation. Realizing this wasn't working the way we wanted, we visited the library. We went online and planned another trip, but this time a little better than the one before. We then traveled to Arizona and began a life there. We found better jobs than before, a better and safer life for our children, and along the way, discovered we could travel beyond what was available to us. We were free from the barrier that we could not make it in another city.

Life isn't perfect, but sometimes through one shortcoming we find something better. Had the negative not occurred, I would not be the person I am today. Through each shortcoming, I was encouraged to be better and not make the same mistakes again, and I don't.

The reason is because I changed how I viewed life today so that tomorrow could be better. I now realize that not completing a successful venture today does not mean it won't be successful tomorrow. Success is a relative term and only applies to the endeavor, not the person. I used the things that would negatively impact others' lives as my encouragement to be a better person. Every day, I make it a point to make a difference in at least one person's life. Because of this, I spend the day looking for an opportunity to make a different person smile and feel good about their situation, whatever it is. Although this may not work for everyone, it is my personal goal and I continually work toward it.

Starting now, I need you to realize that life is about situations. We're not looking for resolutions right now, just understanding the difference between what is situational and what is personal. The only thing we can manage is how we personally respond to each situation. Sometimes all it takes is to pause before reacting and it changes the entire landscape of the situation. The situations that most affected me have been my children, my former spouse, and the health of my parents. How I respond to those situations is the only thing I can control and are the only constants. Outside of that, everything else is a situation. After you understand that everything in life is a situation, you can move forward into what is commonly known as conflict resolution.

You don't actually resolve conflicts in the mental sense. Once an issue becomes a conflict, it is personal and becomes a part of your emotional state. To avoid a conflict, you deal with the situation when it arises. The reason you can't make it personal is because you are not responsible for someone else's emotional state and reactions any more than they are for yours. Any issue, when it occurs, should be dealt with at that moment. No situation should be allowed to affect your entire day. The best point of this is the statement that ends with," … and it ruined my entire day." Why? Because you let someone else's words or actions change how you live your life today. That's it right there. The only person who can affect your day is you, and that is because of how you handle each situation. No situation should linger beyond the moment

You can't become a new person until you are able to close out who you are today. Understanding how to manage situations will always begin with understanding that life is fully and totally about situations. If you run a mile today, you know you aren't running a marathon tomorrow, even if that is the ultimate goal. Because the results aren't instant, there is a tendency to give up or not try. Nothing worth having comes instantly or easily. When a person wins the Nobel Prize, they don't talk about winning the prize. The acceptance speech is about the trials they went through that made it possible to win the Nobel Prize; each situation they encountered and how they overcame it; how many hours they worked in order to find a resolution, and not going to bed until that one item was resolved. The victory was not in the finished product, but in the ability to fight through each shortcoming or challenge and find a resolution. A major victory is the result of many small victories over time.

The expectation is that when people read these pages they will look for every situation where it won't apply to them, because human nature is to naturally look for the negative first, but there isn't a situation that this does not apply to. Successfully raising a child is overcoming all the small challenges and claiming those victories until they reach adulthood and begin their own path to successful life management. The job was to get them through their youth and prepared for life. Afterward, the fight is theirs, not yours, and they have to be allowed to make mistakes so they can grow as you did. Looking at my own life, I know that working in a parts plant does not qualify me for working with a software company, so I studied different books on web development to prepare me for that venture. Once employed with the company; I read and consulted with people who had already accomplished what I was reaching for.

No matter what the situation is, to overcome the shortcomings, one must begin dealing with it today while it is fresh in the mind; while there is still a rational understanding of what did not work and before blaming the shortcoming on what you can't do instead of what you don't know right now. Understanding that is the first step in the building blocks for a better tomorrow. It changes how you approach life and allows you to find a calm that you normally don't experience because you are now dealing with situations when they arise instead of after they have been allowed to fester in your mind and affect your emotional state. You are creating a mindset that you can reach a mental expansion that improves your own quality of life with immediate resolutions.

So what have we learned so far about the opinions that should matter in our lives? First, we learned that the opinions of others should not affect our opinion of ourselves.

We also learned that life is about situations. We understand that even though we have personal relationships, the issues within those relationships are situational and should be approached that way. The love you harbor for someone is personal, but the things that surround your decisions are situational. The first step to keeping matters from becoming personal is to address the situation when it arises.

We also understand that the majority of our shortcomings come from not dealing with the situations when they first arise, thus creating a communication gap when dealing with individuals. The key to conflict resolution is as simple as bridging the educational gap. What do we see when relationships break down? The end result is the only thing people remember. What is actually present is the lack of communication and a failure to seek a resolution to a situation when it arises. One party feels he or she is missing something, but instead of addressing the situation with the other party, the individual or individuals seek the resolution elsewhere, thus creating an even bigger situation. The moment that feeling that something is missing came about, it should have been addressed. If it is not resolved, then the other party should have the option to make a different choice.

Trial and error is the answer for educating ourselves to become stronger and wiser. You know what you want in life, and the only way you can get that is by addressing each situation on the path to that resolution. You may not like what is required during the journey, but the journey is always worth it in the end.

In the end, the building blocks are nothing more than the tools necessary to build a better you. They are not the resolution. They are just part of the source materials for becoming a better you. They are essential because they give you a new way of thinking and approaching your life. Just because you can see the road does not mean you are actually going to travel it. It is still better to know all the necessary materials required before deciding if you are prepared to take the journey. Once you establish what you need, you can move to real-life application and take on the task.

Life is full of examples of people who have overcome difficult lifestyles to create success stories. They generally share the stories, and the response is usually the same for most when they hear them: *Well, they are stronger than I am. Or, well, I tried and didn't get the same breaks they got.* Some may even say they got lucky, which is why they were able to find success. The truth is they changed their mindset and refused to accept the opinions of others who said they would not amount to anything more than the majority of people from that environment or that the feat couldn't be accomplished.

The key factor here is the word *majority*. That means there are many who have made the decision to venture outside the norm and see that they are stronger than the opinions of others. But there are still those who have moved beyond that mental prison to reach for something bigger and better. They were able to establish the building blocks necessary to create a new world for themselves by re-establishing who they were with a strengthened personal and mental foundation.

Our boundaries are limited by what we believe we can accomplish. We believe our accomplishments are limited to what others, over time, have instilled in us as limitations. Those limitations are carried over as a mental vice restricting our drive to do better. That drive to do better is limited by a comfort zone created by a stagnant life, with little to no challenges in our path. We don't have to overcome anything we haven't seen before and therefore are satisfied with not moving forward, or so we think. Yet we complain about the state of our lives because of the success we see of others who have been in far worse situations than we have.

We fail to see that the reason they overcame was because of a drive to be better. They were able to identify the fact that a perceived flaw was nothing more than a negative perception that had been accepted as fact. Those words were used as a driving force behind the desire to succeed at the present venture. All of this was identified in the beginning as the things that needed to change in their lives. Once they were identified, they were able to create an action plan to change how they viewed themselves. It was not important how others viewed them, only how they viewed themselves.

Here is your project. I want you to get your building blocks together. You must start by identifying what you believe are weaknesses in your character. You want to honestly identify what it is about you that you don't like. It could be physical, social, or it could be mental. Either way, you are going to identify all these qualities. Put them down on paper or on your computer.

Next, you want to create a list of the things you want to accomplish. Those items, you want to put into four different sections. You want to label the sections "one month," "three months," "six months," and "a year." Now that they are on two separate sheets of paper, you can look at your goals and what you deem as limitations. Which limitation will keep you from accomplishing which goal?

This is your first building block. You needed to identify what you viewed as a flaw. Now you have the mental limitations written down, which allows you something to focus on. It is your mental and physical checklist. Each time you overcome the mental block, you can check it off the list. I will show you how to overcome them in the next chapter, but for now, you still need to get all of your building blocks in order.

Now you want to go back over your list of mental roadblocks and organize them from which ones are the easiest to identify to the ones that are most complex. The reason for this is when the time comes to begin removing the road blocks, you will begin with the easiest to overcome and work toward the hardest. Generally, the ones easiest to identify are the ones are based on outside sources. The ones where the influences of others are causing the mental conflict are the ones that are most difficult to overcome because they usually are created over long periods of time and continually come into our lives.

The words of discouragement generally come from people we trust, such as friends and family. Many times, they aren't saying these things to hurt us, but instead think they are protecting us from negative emotions caused by the failure to successfully complete a task on the first try. Over time, we use this safety net to determine if the task we wish to take on is worth the effort. We want the result without the effort. I say in most cases because there are still those who will say we are not intelligent enough, not strong enough, or even question our overall physical ability and character. Those too seem to be family members and people we are associated with on a daily basis.

Just because the person giving you the information is close to you does not mean the information is correct. Again, one must consider the source of the information. What has that person who is feeding you the information accomplished that makes the opinion giver an authority on your abilities? Generally, nothing has been accomplished by the person expressing an opinion about your ability that is beyond the scope of what is within your grasp, so the opinion used to belittle the efforts or desires of family members and friends with low self-worth to make them feel better about their lack of successful ventures. Remember, they have to bring you either up or down to less than the level at which they are mentally. They are not better people for it; they are worse. It is an area of needed improvement and something we need to work on in terms of building a new persona and also is another building block within a building block.

The ultimate goal is to create an exercise that allows us to capture and identify every area of needed improvement so we have a resource that shows the area of our own lives we need to improve. We are going to plan a trip to a better tomorrow by revisiting where we are today and how we got here. Using today as a reference point of where we started so when we reach the end of a new road, we can look back and applaud the work that was required to get us to where we are.

The most important part of the exercise is to identify where the negative information is coming from. If it is a person, then we need to identify that person and what it is that the opinion giver does do to make us question our self-worth. We need to review how we feel about ourselves and our ability to complete the tasks we have written down. We must always remember to consider the source of that information. In many instances, we may outgrow the person who attempts to diminish our growth and ability.

Now you have your building blocks. As you write them down, there are going to be some things that you never thought were hindering your life's progression. It could be a source you thought was positive and it turns out that opinions or actions made with good intentions are giving the most negative feedback. Not because the opinion was intended to hold you back, but because a voice of avoiding trying to avoid hardships is simply a negative voice disguised as a positive role model.

NEGATIVE VOICES

Many times in life we find ourselves seeking words of encouragement from friends; family, or peers when we desire to seek out new endeavors. When we get those words, we tend to believe that the information provided was in our best interest and accept it as so. Many times, the person giving the information believes as well that he or she are looking at the best interest of the person he or she are giving the information to, instead of considering the consequences of poor advice.

We're going to explore the information we receive from other sources when dealing with our direction in life. We will use that information as a guideline to turning off the negative voices. Some voices are verbal, while others are mental.

Let's explore a little deeper into the verbal negative voices since they are the most prominent and sometimes the hardest to identify. We will begin with the voices generated from youth to adulthood. Those are the hardest to overcome; the impression they created has become a part of who we are today and have time as an additional factor. Depending on our upbringing and community, they could have been intended for good and unknowingly created a negative outcome.

From childhood, we were told what we could accomplish in life, how smart we were, and how attractive we were. This actually began from birth and continued throughout our development. These words created the groundwork for how we perceive information given to us in our adulthood. If it was given to us in a positive context, we would find ourselves more receptive to the opinions of others and accept the information as positive. If we were in a home or around people who were always negative and were treated differently from other family members, then we would be less likely to take any feedback as positive and thus would have a low self-worth value and be less likely to attempt anything that would stand the risk of imminent failure.

Either way, both impressions will create the negative mental voices that affect our way of thinking today. Because the damage is more severe from the negative reinforcement, we will actually start there. We will look to the source and the information provided. We will also utilize real-life scenarios and go over positive solutions through self-mental recovery methods. The mind is the tool of strength and weakness in people, and now is the time to take control of our most valuable resource.

> One's strength lies in the ability to understand that the mind is the source of life's victories and defeats. Overcoming the thought that we cannot and replacing it with "I will" is the greatest victory one will accomplish.

Children growing up in a home where abuse and alcohol are part of the daily routine are more apt to have very little self-worth. The attitudes of those in the household tend to carry over to the children. The abuse is not limited to the physical; it could also be verbal abuse. A mother or father who continually tells a child he or she will never amount to anything is more damaging than a physical abuser in many cases. Children in some cases are told that they are just like the parent who is not doing anything positive in their life and therefore should expect no better results.

These children will either become very reclusive and uninvolved or will lash out and become a part of what they are a victim to. They will verbally abuse their siblings and friends as well because the abuse has become a part of their normal environment. The abuse can, and in many cases does, involve other family members such as a sibling, also telling the victim that he or she is of little worth. Because it is a normal pattern for the victim to receive such abuse, the victims are less likely to expect anything better from outside sources and will limit what they feel they can accomplish or attempt to avoid receiving more ridicule if abuse victims are not immediately successful in their venture. The self-worth is gone, and therefore the victims look to accept what life gives them instead of reaching for what they cannot readily see. The abuse victims' dreams are usually simple, and they only seek relief from those vices that burden them mentally. The mental damage is unnerving to those who have never experienced it, and they tend to eventually add to the rhetoric instead of helping the abuse victim to overcome it. We will visit this later, but for now, we will focus on what negative impact this type of abuse from youth does and ways to overcome it.

Verbal abuse is as common as a change in the weather. No one is immune to it, and the sources vary. The most common and most damaging, as stated previously, come from immediate family members, beginning in a person's youth. A child who has been a victim of verbal abuse usually began seeing it from one parent to another parent and eventually watched it trickle down to them.

As the child grows older and the confidence diminishes, the abuse tends to get worse due to the lack of motivation to venture outside the norm to accomplish new feats or establish new goals. Now the attacks go toward not only what the child did in his or her past, but how limited the child will be in terms of the success their future will hold. There is a tendency to also attack the intelligence of said child. Siblings have a tendency to get involved, which can create a totally defeated mentality.

This type of defeated mentality can lead to one of two directions. We see children led into bad social circles because they seek the comfort of those from similar back grounds. They seek comfort through associations with people who give them the positive attention they lacked during their early developmental years.

These are groups not seeking social acceptance. They look for their own path and look for nothing beyond what that group offers. They have no drive to be anything other than what the group offers as acceptable. There is no future in being the follower in a group of people who don't desire to accomplish anything. If someone in the group accomplishes something exceptional, the aspiring individuals are viewed in their own social circle as trying to be better than everyone else and treated as an outsider.

So the question now is how do you overcome those negative outside voices to reach greater heights? The first thing is no different than what has been stated previously. We must first consider the source of the information. What did the person who gave you negative feedback accomplish that makes the person an authority on your life direction? Sometimes it is hard to escape from that mental prison because some of those individuals will tell you they just don't want you to get hurt and actually have good intentions when they speak regarding your goals and aspirations. They will tell you of how society views you because you are a part of that group and say that you are socially unacceptable. If you aspire to accomplish something great and are part of a group that is attempting to deter you from reaching those heights, then you may be a part of the wrong social group. Your friends would encourage you to do better, not discourage you from expanding into new areas.

> Good intentions from a bad source generally produce poor results.

By working outside of the restrictive mental boundaries set by your family or associates, you are creating an opportunity within yourself to be an inspiration to others within that group. You came from the same restrictive society and rose above it because you found a way to turn off and tune out the negative voices. You have to look beyond today in order to see that tomorrow will come. You have to venture out to new boundaries in order to open up the future opportunities.

I admit it is difficult to overcome the negative voices of our established inner circles, because those relationships have been established over time and the intentions are generally meant to be good-natured. Sometimes they are good intentions without merit, thus creating an acceptance of a negative voice over a growth opportunity. Once we accept an opinion as fact, we then establish a pattern of doing the same things we always do without taking risks that could lead to the fulfillment of our dreams, therefore declining to do what is necessary for completing our ultimate goal. Consider the source in regard to what we can and cannot accomplish. If you have a parent who has had one failed relationship after another, that parent is probably not the best resource for relational advice. If the person you get advice from is verbally and mentally abusive, that individual is definitely not the best person to share your life's dreams with. The opinion giver will only tell you that you cannot accomplish those feats you desire to accomplish.

To change tomorrow, we have to take actions today. Again, no major victory comes without a lot of small victories. Everything has to go through the necessary steps in order to have completion of the entire task. Negative voices are no different. If someone tells you that you're a failure and you never seem to reach you ultimate goal, you begin to believe you're a failure and give up on your dreams. The problem wasn't in the person telling you that you couldn't attain new heights; the problem was you eventually believed it. People are entitled to their opinions, and you're entitled to realize that they have no merit in your life.

In the proper perspective, let's now solve this problem overall. Regardless of the source of the negative voice, whether it was an influential adult making negative statements during your childhood or someone with good intentions giving bad advice, the information or statements they provided were nothing more than a negative influence or opinion. The source of the negative voice, in actuality, was your own mind. It was the acceptance of that influence that discouraged our dreams, hopes, or desires to be better tomorrow than we are today, not the fact that the statement or comment was made. We must then look in the mirror so we can see the true source of the negative voices. It is in us that the voices exist and in us that we must purge the voices. The only opinion that should matter in our lives is our own.

So let's begin the healing and restoration process. People in all phases of our lives have accomplished or overcome different obstacles, which we can use as examples and resources to avoid repeating the same errors they made along the way. If they haven't overcome something, then we can still use where they are today to encourage us to take a different direction tomorrow. Either way, we now have a way of using this information to our own benefit.

In order for other people's experiences to make a difference, we must first realize that in the end our own opinion is the strength to our inspiration and guidance to be better. That opinion we have of ourselves has to be positive in order for us to have the desire to accomplish anything. If you don't have faith in yourself, then obviously, no one else will. So that, today, is your first step to change the way you view yourself.

We will start with an obvious question and move to the very simple answer within our solution cycle. How do I change how I see myself? This, although it seems simple in words, is the more difficult part of what we are trying to accompli sh. For every shortcoming we have, I can guarantee there is something positive about ourselves that we can see. It is not possible to have a negative solution without a positive. The opposite of everything exists. That includes what the mind perceives as possible. You may believe you can't accomplish something, but in order to believe that, you first must dream of accomplishing it.

Let's focus on our positive traits first. What are the things people say about you that are positive? Identify what they say and then consider the source. Are they people with good moral values and ideals? Do they show continual progress in their own lives? During the most trying of times, do they appear in control and able to make sound decisions? If yes, then use that opinion as a source of strength. These people may not know everything about you, but at the same time, apparently they see more good in you than you do in yourself. Sit down with them and have them validate for you why they feel that way about you. You may be surprised that you have made a difference to them by something you do daily.

Anything positive in your life is now your major source of inspiration. Also, the words of the person who believes in your ability and always has a positive word of encouragement for you when you feel the worst about yourself are also an excellent source of inspiration. Whenever you have a negative thought, think of those positive things or what that person who always encourage you would say at this moment. The idea is to develop a new way of thinking and managing the negative voices.

Regardless of the number of successful endeavors you have, you will always have negative voices. How you manage them dictates you path toward your dream fulfillment. If you manage them well, then you will find yourself living a peaceful existence and continually growing and expanding your world. If not, then you will have high-stress moments and harbor doubts about you own ability. You will refuse new ventures because you will carry the concern of what someone else would think of you if it is not a successful endeavor. In many cases, you will feel that you would disappoint a parent, spouse, or your children if you do not successfully complete the task. Understand the words in that last sentence, because they are very important. If you fail to successfully complete a task, disappointment may come to you as a negative voice.

Failure is a relative term, just like the word success. Relative terms do not apply to anything that can evolve over time.

If you have the ability to make a decision to do something different during the cycle of life, whether it is physical or mental, then relative terms do not apply. You change daily, both mentally and physically, regardless of what happened the previous day.

That is the reason I do not--let me say that again--I do not use the terms "success" or "fail" when referring to people's lives. The only thing a person can actually succeed at is the completion of the cycle of life. Whether long or short, the lifecycle will be successfully completed. That's it, and once you realize that, the process of eliminating negative voices becomes easier. You will now understand that only the endeavor fails, not the person.

At any age, a person can go back to school and gain a degree in a different field. That is a successful endeavor that now allows a person to change careers. If the individual going back to school doesn't complete the courses necessary to gain the degree, the endeavor is still successful because he gained additional knowledge. But with the new knowledge, he or she will now have changed the way things are seen in regard to life as well. Your mind is ever evolving. The more valid information you provide you mind with, the more you expand your areas of opportunity. This goes along the lines of what we discussed the chapter "Understanding the Development of New Boundaries" in regarding people venturing out farther to eventually open up the entire world to themselves.

No statement can be made without validation; otherwise it is nothing more than an opinion. So here is the validation to the facts regarding success and failure in the relative sense. When you envision yourself completing a

task, is it the task that gets completed, or is it the person becoming complete? Keep in mind that completion is a term meaning finality. You're completing a task; therefore, *you* have not been completed, but the task has. Thus, you have successfully completed a task or venture. In essence, you are not successful, but instead you have been successful at completing a task and have successfully expanded your mental world. You have the ability to take on a new task because you are not complete.

If success is relative, then would not its opposite also be relative? If you attempt a venture and are unable to complete it due to either some miscalculations or even due to lack of knowledge regarding the task requirements, wouldn't the question remain the same as with success in regard to failure? Are you not a success, or were you just not successful at the completion of a task? The task can still be completed; thus it can still have a successful ending. You have still successfully expanded the amount of knowledge you have about the subject. You learned what does not work along the way to the ultimate conclusion. The only requirement is that you need more education regarding the task, which requires more mental evolution so you can alter the outcome. The benefit is that due to you gaining that additional knowledge, you've now expanded your boundaries once again.

Why isn't our way of thinking the same about everything? Perception is what drives decision-making, not knowledge, which is the opposite of what it should be. People study for tests and question if they have the correct answers. Not because they don't have the information, but instead they have the perception that it could be wrong because human nature accepts the negative over the positive.

From youth, we are trained to view the negative over the positive, and it is time to change that thought process as well. It will change one's quality of life if we as people can see the positive results in life and work toward them. To overcome them, we must first realize our limitations and change those limitations into positive resources. We do that by educating ourselves about the things we have limited knowledge about. If you want to know about a different job at your workplace, then you ask someone in that position to find out what they had to accomplish to reach those heights. Understand where the problems lie and what areas they struggled in and how they overcame them so you can avoid the same mistakes.

Now that you've changed the terrain, you can begin to change the battle. The knowledge you have now is that your mind is the actual battlefield for growth and enhancement in life. Your mind is the terrain, and you now have the resource to change the nature of the battle, because it will now be fought on your terms. The greatest weapon we have in order to overcome the negative voices is the fact that the only voices we hear that determine decision-making are our own.

It's time to look back once again to the next phase of development in getting rid of the negative voices. It goes back to considering the source. This is the information we have been receiving and who we're receiving it from. Generally, anything positive we want to accomplish is discouraged by the voice of a person or persons who have accomplished nothing on their own, or very little. They are fighting the same internal voices you are and have surrendered to them and, in what they think is an effort to protect you, they try to discourage you from the risk of not successfully completing a task they determined too difficult for them. This is actually very damaging to one's mental makeup because these are words from people who actually care for us and have attempted what you are now attempting. These are friends and loved ones who have accomplished little and see us with the same eyes they see themselves with. The negative is in the fact that if they don't believe you can accomplish it because they couldn't, then they are actually seeing themselves as having a higher mental makeup than you. If they didn't, then they would not deem it necessary to advise you against it. They would assume with your advanced or equal knowledge that you could perceive the risks without outside influence. Understand the intentions are good, but the source is not.

When listening to others, we must always consider the source of the information. Is the source a combative person who seems to never want anyone to do better than them? They will discourage you just to ensure that they have accomplished more than those around them. They never want you to do something they haven't been able to accomplish. These people are easily identified because if you share information or a story with them, they will have a story to follow yours that has either a greater tragedy or a brighter ending.

Generally, you don't want to share your goals with these individuals, because they will attempt to accomplish your dreams only to say they did it first. They will discourage you if it will give you something they have not been able to accomplish, because it would require you to overcome something they weren't willing to put in the effort to overcome themselves. You can share the success, but not the dream, if you want to avoid the negative influence. In many cases, these relationships don't last very long once we begin to accomplish greater things in life because these individuals tend to add and remove people from their social circles frequently, based on how their associates are doing in life.

They mask the negative influence with what appear to be good intentions. They tell you about how bad it was for them when they tried it or how unrealistic it is for you to go beyond where you are because of your level of education. Or they remind you of how many more people are more qualified than you are. The fact behind that is the qualification for that is you and what effort you're willing to put forth to make you more qualified than them. Education and experience go a long way to leveling the playing field. The only time you're not up to a task is when you accept the thought that you're not as factual. At all other times, you are just as exceptional as the next person.

> The greatest mind is the mind that accepts its limitations as challenges to expand knowledge instead of an acknowledgment of defeat.

The strength of your success will always lie in your willingness to expand your knowledge base. No negative voice can be heard over the validation of evidence to the contrary. Once you understand the difference between the completion of a task and the fact that not completing it is the amount of information one possesses, you will be able to accomplish anything you desire because you will always look to expand your knowledge to get you there. Utilize your resources in order to gain the information necessary to reach your goals. To overcome anything negative, one must have evidence that it is not a fact that is unattainable. That evidence is in the knowledge you can gain to the contrary. Look to those who have already overcome those same hurdles you must now clear in order to accomplish your goal. You must always remember that every major victory is the result of a lot of small ones. The best way to discourage a person from being a negative influence to you is to be able to say to the opinion giver, "I've already done it." The conversation should begin with "I wanted to." Then you make the statement of what you wanted to accomplish. The individual expressing the opinion to you will attempt the negative influencing process, and when they finish you can close with, "I've already done it. I just wanted to share it with you."

The last and most difficult negative influences in our lives are the ones that began in our youth. This is generally from parents or siblings. It generally is in some form of verbal abuse but in some cases is actually stated with good intentions. Verbal abuse generally starts with a parent telling a child that he or she has little self-worth. The child's intelligence and decision-making are put into question. And he or she is told that very little will be accomplished in life, and it usually goes over a long period of time. That child is made to feel inferior mentally to other children or siblings because he or she may have to work harder at something or could have physical differences.

We can't choose our parents or siblings, but we can choose our friends and direction we want to travel in life. Again, from a young age we are encouraged by society to trust the sources of information inside of our structured environment. Although it may not have the best structure in some cases, the home is still a structured environment. Structure is nothing more than a foundation established for development during anything's pre-developmental stages. Our social skills are developed from this environment, which establishes our early social circles and confidence. That confidence is what gives credence to the negative voices within us. If your early development comes from a home life that is encouraging as well as nurturing, then you will hold the control early on over the negative voices because you will be given the push necessary early to overcome obstacles. If they are negative, you will tend to either be reclusive or find your own comfort zone and not reach beyond it due to the desire to not seek the negative responses that were learned from the early development phase of life.

A poor foundation develops a person's desire to or excuse for not wanting to disappoint someone in their life. In some cases, parents are the source of this mental choice. They may tell you stories of how they struggled to reach where they are and don't want you to go through what they went through. The intentions are good natured but negative. You have to choose your own path in life, have your own dreams, and be allowed to make mistakes along the way that you can learn and grow from. The education is in the overcoming, not in the not doing. If you never try to accomplish anything new, how do you know you can't accomplish it? The failure is not in the person, because you cannot fail in life; you can only fail to try. The failure is in the decision made to not try. The same parent who loves you enough to try to protect you will love you just as much for accomplishing a feat they were not able to accomplish.

No matter what or who the source is, the ultimate decision for change still lies within you. But you first must reinforce the foundation of your mind's understanding of the education in trial and error. That begins with the negative voices that will continually try to tear down what you are trying to build within yourself. In order to accomplish that, one must first have a strong foundation, and that foundation will always be how we view ourselves. How you view yourself determines your ability to overcome obstacles. This determines how you process information and accept risk. If you think and live in the negative, then you will view things with the negative possibilities first. That fear of failing to complete that goal limits our drive to push forward when obstacles occur.

Regardless of children's upbringing, when they are away from home, they always seem to try the things their parents restricted them from doing in their youth. The thought that their parent(s) were only attempting to keep the children in question from having fun came into play. But the reality was that the parent(s) had already traveled that road and knew what the pitfalls were. They were successful in completing the transition from childhood into adulthood. They were the resource that could have helped that child avoid the same influences that slowed their own progression. All children don't fall into those traps, though.

We must rid ourselves of everything in our lives that negatively impacts our way of thinking and make the choice to act on a situation instead of remaining stagnant and refusing growth. That includes the people who don't provide any positive feedback into our well-being. A misguided friend who provides misguided advice is just as bad as a mate who is guilty of the same thing. In some situations one person's perception of fact is no more than an accepted truth without the benefit of factual information, making the perception nothing more than an opinion. It is always hard to let our associates that we've know for a long time go by the wayside. Just as a person recovering from drugs or alcoholism needs to get away from the people who encouraged that type of lifestyle, the same rules apply to people who had or have low self-worth. Getting those people who discourage personal mental growth out of your life so that you can have a better tomorrow is essential. It is a part of dealing with a situation and becoming more educated.

Where family is concerned, you may not want to sever the relationship, but you still must consider the source of information. If anything, their negative influence should be used as a springboard to success. Human nature is to view the negative over the positive, and it is a shared quality. It is one that others view their past without looking to their future. Don't allow them to blame the fact that they became a parent as an excuse for not doing more with their lives. Every day single parents go back to school so they can provide a better life for their families. Every day someone that society deemed unable to be productive reaches new heights and becomes part of the so-called success stories.

These aren't success stories. They are simply people rising above the negative voices to see something brighter and taking the necessary steps to make it a reality. Think of how many people who were homeless now own businesses and their own homes.

On more than one occasion I was invited to a business seminar and I listened to individuals speak of needing to move in with parents, living in cars or with friends, waiting for the business ventures they were involved with to show positive results. The faith in the business and the faith they had in the decisions they made to work the business systems eventually paid dividends. Clearly, them standing at the podium speaking of it shows that through drive, faith, and education, the goals they set came to fruition.

The most recent example of this was sitting in on a seminar sponsored by a person who learned how to run a home business from Dexter Yeager. I listened to all that was overcome from being homeless and living with parents to becoming a millionaire over the next ten years. The realization is that it didn't happen overnight, but through patience and dedication the eventual goal was accomplished. They had two choices: give up and accept the fate of homelessness like so many others, or rise above it and take on the challenges before them to have a brighter tomorrow.

It's time to silence the negative voices and accept the responsibility of our own decision-making. We need to rid ourselves of the negative influences that have hindered our mind's development. We need to look at our own positives instead of at what we perceive as negative in our lives. We need to get educated on the things necessary for our future development and growth. And we need to consider the source of the negative influences in our lives. In the end, we need to understand that it is our own mind that hinders us and the decisions of our lives are our own responsibility, not someone else's. They can share their opinion, but it is simply that: their opinion, not yours, and that is the key point to remember at all times. Everyone is entitled to have an opinion. We have to remember that an opinion is a statement without fact. It is what they think or perceive as true but without relevant facts to back it up, and it means nothing more than that. At that point it is nothing more than a theory. When you hear an opinion you always reserve the right to ask them a simple question: "Have you tried it?" If the answer is no, then a second qualifying question should arise. "If you haven't tried it, then how do you know it is not possible?"

It's time for you to gain control of your life by first establishing building blocks and then getting rid of the negative voices. Thinking positive is the foundation for being positive. Once you have the positive mindset, you can then begin setting attainable goals.

CREATING THE ATTAINABLE GOAL

Once we change our way of thinking about ourselves, our goals have a tendency to change in accordance with that way of thinking as well. We envision ourselves reaching levels of greatness we never even considered an option before. In many cases, based on the knowledge we have, those dreams would be beyond our scope of rational thought. It's not that they are not attainable goals. They are only unattainable with the tools and information we have available to us at the time.

Every new venture is about taking the necessary steps to make a goal or dream become a reality. We need to be able to validate whatever it is we desire to do with our lives with the knowledge necessary to make it become a reality. The avenues for success do not solely lie inside a book or classroom. We have talked about utilizing resources, and now we will put those resources to work for our development. Resources are nothing more than sources of knowledge utilized in the quest to complete a task. That includes people who have already had success in the area where we are now about to venture.

The idea of an attainable goal is not limited to one's ability, but instead to one's ability to handle the task at hand based on the information and skills they possess. You can have the goal to reach a certain level in anything in life. What is important is to understand what is required to make the dream a reality.

To become a college graduate, a person must first decide that he or she wants to go to college. Once the individuals have determined that furthering their education is the goal, they must follow some necessary steps to get there. From the beginning, he or she had to establish a good foundation. That foundation began in the early stages of school. As a child, that person had to go to school each day. Learn to establish good study habits. The reason your homework was or is essential is because in college there is no one over your shoulder making sure the work gets done. There are no late assignments that can be made up later. Either you did the work or you didn't. It became essential to develop positive habits along the way.

So you graduate from preschool and your educational foundation is established. You learned to read and write. You learned your colors and how to count. You learned how to add and subtract, divide and multiply. Everything essential to graduate from elementary school and move to junior high, you learned in elementary school. The same rules applied in junior high to move to high school. You received more homework in more classes. Teachers provided more organized lesson plans, and you learned better study habits. This prepared you for high school, and high school is supposed to prepare you for college. Although you may have had help in high school, the habits were established by you, and those habits created an opportunity for a brighter future if you mentally prepared for it. Graduation day from college is a great achievement but is only the beginning, because once you complete it, you need to then focus on getting a good job. You successfully completed a task and expanded into new areas in your life and then were able to set your sights on venturing out even farther.

For each major victory, look over the landscape of the previous paragraph, because it required a lot of small victories to get there. So an attainable goal is nothing more than a small victory in the scheme of fulfilling the ultimate dream. To get there one must first understand the fundamental values that are necessary in a person who dares to take on the challenge of accomplishing something beyond his or her immediate grasp.

Excuses will come to the forefront. Every person who has accomplished anything of value had to overcome the "tomorrow excuse syndrome." Remember what was stated previously about the word *tomorrow*. The greatest excuse word used is tomorrow. Why do today what you can put off until tomorrow? Realistically, tomorrow will become nothing more than a catchphrase for "I never planned to do it anyway." More times than not, the term "I'll do it tomorrow" becomes a never-ending cycle of excuses.

This is the reason goals should be realistic. You have an ultimate goal, but you take it one step at a time. Step one is to actually have an ultimate goal. If you have no destination, then you have no reason to plan a trip. We must decide what it is we would like to accomplish in the long term. It doesn't matter what the desire is, just what it is we would ultimately like to realistically accomplish. Call it a goal or a dream, but as long as it is something that is attainable over time with the proper skills and education, then it is okay to reach for it. You must understand that it is a long-term goal and may not be within reach in the near future but may require work and planning.

Once you have established what it is you would ultimately like to accomplish, it is necessary to look at the skills you currently possess and which ones are required for that task to be completed. Each skill set you don't currently possess is considered an educational opportunity. You must then look to your resources in order to accommodate those steps, whether you need to go back to school, read for additional knowledge, look up information on the Internet, at the library or at home, or ask someone who has already accomplished what you're trying to accomplish. The additional knowledge is essential not only to your mental growth, but it is also an expansion of the world you're opening to yourself and a victory in your life.

With each successful venture, you will experience a growth in your confidence. You will feel different about yourself and the life you currently live. You will also be able to see yourself getting closer to your ultimate dream.

Understand that completing the first task should not be viewed as just finishing a phase or part of anything. It is a victory because you have accomplished something you never considered attempting before. Your world has grown and your vision is now broader. What seemed out of your scope is now part of your everyday life.

> To try is an accomplishment; to succeed is a victory.

Every victory requires trials. With every trial comes the risk of error. Thus the term "trial and error" becomes a life reality and an education. No great feat is accomplished without successfully overcoming some trials along the way. The greater the victory, the greater the trials we must overcome. The greater the trials we overcome, the sweeter the ultimate victory feels.

What gives us the ability to overcome the trials placed before us is the preparation along the way. We prepared our mind to understand that our own opinion is the only one that matters. That negative voices are simply accepting as fact opinions that we are less than what we strive to be. That negative influences have no place in our lives and can now be used as fuel to inspire successful completion of our endeavors. We understand that opinions belong to the people who are giving them and are not essential to our daily thoughts. We will consider the source of information pertaining to what we can and cannot successfully accomplish in our lives and that each phase of life and growth began with building blocks and foundation. The foundation was and is in our minds, not our bodies.

It is not a necessity to choose any particular goal to address first. Realistically, you should be picking your goal based on which one will get you the biggest reward for the least amount of work. The reason is even though you know it is to build your confidence in yourself, you must still establish the fact that you have the ability to move forward. It also creates the habit of completing tasks you start.

Your history of completion was established long ago, and if there was a history of successful completion, then you would already have achieved your goals in life and would be working on goals you never imagined. The most basic characteristic in people is their willingness to surrender to negative voices and influences. Regardless of how many successful endeavors you have completed, the history shows there are more endeavors that you have not fulfilled than that you actually have. That is because, as stated previously, human nature is to focus on the negative over the positive.

So completion of the easier undertakings first creates the habit of completion. Once that foundation is established, it will become harder for a person to surrender to those voices, whether they are inside or outside. Those voices gain empowerment each time we decide that an undertaking is either too difficult or that we do not have the time today and will take care of it tomorrow. We must find a way to break the yoke of empowerment before we can successfully complete even the simplest of goals.

Just like completing college courses to gain a degree in a specific field, there is no requirement for what goes first. You know from the very beginning what courses are required for you to gain your degree. The great thing is your undergraduate courses are not required to be completed in any specific order. The reason they are not is because if you begin with the easier courses, you are able to establish greater confidence in yourself. You also learn how to generate good habits that will make the harder courses easier to manage. You learn to manage time both for your education and social life, which gives you the balance necessary to not suffer mental breakdowns. It is imperative that we understand that life requires a balance to avoid frustrations that go along with trial and error.

The tendency is to always provide information to others on how to complete certain tasks, but this is generally done without having completed them on our own. Self-fulfilling goals are generally the hardest ones to complete. This is why it is essential to change the way you view yourself before undertaking such tasks.

Here is a perfect example of how the majority of people surrender to negative voices, which then becomes a part of their nature and environment. Companies have made billions of dollars selling the concept of dietary pills. Not that diet pills don't provide an immediate result, but because human nature is to take the easy path to something instead of taking on the challenges required for a permanent solution, the quick fix generates an immediate result with negative repercussions. People start and stop diets all the time, and each time it is a little harder to regain the previous results because you've already surrendered the effort previously. So we sell ourselves on the fact that we're happy with who we are and what we've accomplished and therefore, stop trying. Then we become critical of people who work out all the time or aspire to complete greater things in their own lives. We attempt to justify our reasoning for not continuing those diets because we don't have time or can't afford the plan. The best excuse for not remaining or starting a diet is this one: "I will make dieting a part of my New Year's resolution. "The New Year's excuse is another version of the tomorrow concept.

Now that we have the excuses, let's identify the human quality we use to validate these statements. We have to keep in mind that human nature is to focus on the negative over the positive. The reason this is so important is because we look at ourselves and see the areas we would like to improve upon in our lives. If women believed they were totally beautiful they would never wear makeup, because they would realize they didn't need it. So they use the excuse that it enhances their natural beauty. The reality is that it alters the natural appearance to give the illusion that they have more depth to their face, hair, or fingers than what is naturally there. It doesn't make them any more beautiful than they were before; it just changes the landscape of what you can see. The same rules do not apply to physical fitness and the mind. You cannot hide who you are in regard to your physical conditioning and appearance any more than you can hide the amount of education you have. There's no cream or polish you can put on in the morning or at night that will change your physical makeup and appearance. But even the person who does work out continually finds different things in his or her physical makeup that he or she is attempting to improve upon. It's not bad to want to look or feel better about yourself. The error is in not being honest with yourself about the reason you're doing it. If you're doing it for any reason other than personal satisfaction, then you're doing it for the wrong reason and will never find the resolution you desire.

Dietary companies exist because people, by nature, do not commit themselves to a daily ritual of physical fitness. They say they don't have time to do it. Time is always the excuse used to avoid taking action on anything in life. "I don't have the money to join the gym" is still an excuse to not undertake the task. The negative voice wins again, because the fact is you could have started at home. The reason the negative voice has so much validity with us is because we're doing things for the wrong reasons. The changes made are generally made to satisfy others' opinions or views of us. Your satisfaction comes when you do it for yourself. Because you see something you want and you take the necessary steps to attain it, your level of satisfaction is greater.

I use exercise as the core example because it is the one area of life where the majority of people quit and then make an excuse to validate the reason for not doing it. It's a statement without validation. If you have time to watch television, then you have time to complete a workout during the show. Thirty minutes per day, three days a week dedicated to physical health creates a new habit of completion. But excuses always seem to come into play. A lot of parents use the excuse that it is too much of an undertaking because they have kids and they take all their time or they are in the way so they can't finish the workout. The amazing thing is if you're doing a workout video and you bring small children into the room, you will find that they will attempt to do it as well.

I used a Billy Blanks workout video to test the theory. The children under twelve in my home all got involved in doing the workout as well. To them, it was fun, just as it is for the people who do it on a regular basis. It is also quality time spent with the kids. In the end, they helped you get into shape and you helped them establish at an early age the importance of fitness. You have now replaced a negative idea with a positive habit.

Getting back to the idea of why diet companies exist and are successful. The majority of their customer base is from repeat business. People take pills that promise to help them lose weight. A pill is not a meal and does not replace the necessary nutrition for daily functioning. But people do it because they don't want to take the tougher road of actually accomplishing a goal with the individual victories accomplished through the different workouts. If they don't see an instant result from working out, they quit because they don't believe it works. The reality is you will get out of it what you put into it. People who work out and eat right sleep better, are able to manage stress better, and ultimately feel better. They have higher self-esteem than those who do not commit to the same daily rituals. Your mind's development is just as important as that of your body. The same rules apply. What you put into it is what you will eventually get out of it.

If you don't use and condition your mind, then clearly you're not going to get the full benefit of what it can do for you. Your mental health is essential to you successfully undertaking and completing tasks. Your desire to accomplish a goal is based on how you condition your mind for such undertakings. Create habits of completion so that they become second nature in your mind. Begin by doing them for the right reason, and that reason is personal growth and expansion of mental boundaries.

Here's the approach I have adopted. What is the point of starting it if I don't intend on finishing it? I am not a fan of "what ifs" and neither should you be. I don't intend to one day say, "What if I had finished doing something, where would I be today?" I understand that not getting the desired result does not mean the task is not completed, only that the result is different than what I wanted. You can undertake the task again with more information and change the result, but completion will always be the end result. Instead, I have created habits of completion, so I don't need a substitute or supplement to cheat my way to a conclusion. Instead, I get the full value of completion because I did it myself through education and hard work. I work out consistently, mentally and physically, so that my mind and body operate at their highest levels all of the time. "I am getting the most value out of me" is the concept I will continually live by, and I challenge everyone around me to do the same thing.

Some people will see your constant improvement and respond with negative comments. As you progress in your endeavors, you will find that more people are critical of your growth. Those comments are your badges of honor and should be treated as compliments. If you go back to school and get an A on an exam, it's an accomplishment. When someone comments that it is only one test, that is a notification of advancement. The comment was meant in a negative sense, but realistically was the acknowledgment that you are on the path to a new victory. You can actually thank them for making the statement.

Of course, the people who truly care for you will compliment your success as well, but they are your natural support system. Sometimes, in spite of your shortcomings, they tend to still provide positive feedback. Sadly, that is not always what is best for you, but they are attempting to ensure that you keep a positive outlook. The truth is better because it allows you to see yourself from another view, and then, if their thoughts can be validated, it gives you a new challenge. Creating new goals inside of existing goals helps increase the level of satisfaction in the end. We do always want to remember when we receive feedback that through it all, we still need to consider the source.

The ability to define a realistic goal over an unrealistic dream is essential as well. No one wants to be disappointed because he or she put in all of the work to fulfill multiple goals when the ultimate goal was never within reach. Look at the basic requirements necessary for the ultimate goal before deciding to undertake the job of fulfilling all the underlying requirements. Look to the small victories in cases like this because the education you receive expands your environment and still constitutes a victory.

What you can control is your drive and desire to complete the tasks that are before you. What you don't control is what requirements someone else has put in place in addition to the skills that you have or will be developing. A person with vision restrictions can learn to fly a plane but should not have the ultimate goal of becoming a fighter pilot. Learning to fly is your victory. It's not realistic to have poor vision and want to be a fighter pilot, but it doesn't take away from the accomplishment of learning to fly a plane.

You must be honest about your restrictions before you attempt to undertake a major task to avoid being discouraged in the future. If you're the only person with a master's degree in business management with a company but the company is privately owned and the owner's son is your competition for an executive position within the company carrying the family name, you can't be disappointed in the fact that he gets the job over you. That is something beyond your control. It doesn't make your degree any less important, and you can still establish yourself as essential to that company. If you desire the position the son received, then it may be necessary to strengthen your skills where you are and look for the opportunity elsewhere.

Your value is in your ability to establish realistic goals in the scope of what is available to you. Again, you gained the knowledge to complete a certain reasonable goal. Once you've successfully completed the endeavor you desired, you can change your focus to something greater. Just because one thing has been completed does not mean there isn't another undertaking available.

What we would like to do is avoid the pitfalls that come with accomplishment. Once a goal is reached, people become stagnant in their lives. They forget that mental growth was available because they changed their way of thinking to get there. Now they fall back into that old way of thinking and no longer look to that growth but instead rest on their laurels. They have gained strength from the victory over the negative voices. They may no longer be victim to the control over them but may become victim to human nature. They see a major victory as a successful life, and it is nothing more than the successful completion of a task. The cycle of life isn't complete; only one ultimate goal was reached on a list of many.

People don't realize that the most criticized business is the one whose business model is duplicated the most. Without going into the model and only addressing the business itself, we will address a Michigan-based company to make a closing point to setting goals. Their successful business model is repeated and the company is never credited with creating or mastering it.

Many people have the desire to be financially independent. They come up with business plans and ideas and begin to work toward them. They look at other successful companies' business models and attempt to duplicate those successful business strategies. Meanwhile, the people who have created the core of that model continue to evolve, not only with their business concept, but in the products or services that they offer as well. They have reached a level of corporate success and changed their focus to improve even upon that. The mind is no different, but in the case I'm making, no one is immune from this development.

If you desire to be successful, look at the most successful business model available. Not only does the model apply to business, but it also applies to how you can manage your life and ideas. If duplicated in the same format that the founders established, you will find not only the success that you desire for each endeavor, but you will also find satisfaction in doing it the right way for the right reason.

The idea for a successful society is to be self-sufficient. If you are the producer of a something and you don't support it, then you are doomed for a failed business endeavor. If you have an idea and share the concept with others but never undertake it yourself, you only have yourself to blame for not finding the success someone else has encountered. Your mind and body are your business, and each endeavor is for the betterment of that business. Your ideas are nothing more than business strategies designed to improve your business.

When you have an idea or dream and you fail to take action to make that dream a reality, the loss is yours, not anyone else's. No one else is to blame for you not taking action. No one can be blamed for you not educating yourself and using your available resources to reach that ultimate goal but you. Anything someone says in relation to what you can accomplish is nothing but an opinion because there is no validation to support such a statement. How can you know if you can complete something if you've never attempted it? Even if you have attempted to complete it, you still need to verify how much information you had in order to complete it to your own satisfaction. What steps were required in order for that dream to become a reality? If you didn't successfully complete the undertaking, then you also have to look to the steps you either took shortcuts on or skipped. If you didn't skip steps or take shortcuts, then what information did you lack in the process?

To verify the best business concept available with the best opportunity for success, if followed, is available through research. If you want to begin a life of successful endeavors, you must first learn to establish the building blocks for the necessary mental development. Then you can utilize your resources to attain them.

If everyone in America followed the business concept I spoke of earlier and made it generational, not only would they be self-sufficient, but they would also be millionaires within five years. Even with all the negative comments regarding the business, it still thrives and still produces more legitimate millionaires than any other. The founders are billionaires and continue to thrive and help others become successful, even today, because they desired to help others become self-sufficient. From the small town of Ada, Michigan, a small business has become a global financial leader. With all the criticism they receive, they still do nothing but grow and develop. With each successful endeavor, they reach beyond into new territories. The same way all people who aspire to do better in life can continue to grow and develop.

If you don't support yourself, why should anyone else? The establishment of good habits is essential to growth in life. Your life and mental makeup are your business. Your greatest resource is your mind because it is the one thing you can gain control of in order to influence everything else you do. Criticism is nothing more than notifications of successful or impending victories. But if you don't support yourself, you will have one endeavor after another that is not completed to your satisfaction, and what should have been victories for you will instead be victories for the negative voices.

Reasonable goals are always going to be the hardest concept to develop because of the natural desire to accomplish more than those who came before us. Human nature is to think bigger following any victory. The first time someone scores the winning basket in a basketball game in their youth, they begin to envision making the shot to win the NBA title. Those who were witness to that success become critical of that shot. Not because it wasn't impressive but because they were not the ones to reach that level of successful completion. They don't see that being on the team made them a part of the conclusion. So they demean every aspect of what that person did leading up to that shot, until that person questions his or her own ability or accepts that as nothing more than just one shot. It wasn't just one made basket, but instead it was a milestone on the road to many.

The people who accomplish great things look to improve the things that others were critical of. The attainable goals are those that led to that one moment of glory. If you've shown flashes of greatness at times, then guess what? That greatness is always there; you just have to make it a part of your everyday routine.

Michael Jordan was considered great not because of the overall accomplishments but instead because they were a part of his everyday ritual. All people were able to see were the end results of his hard work. No one was able to see the conditioning and the mental preparation. They forget he missed more game winning shots than he made in his career. But if you look at what he did between the opening tap of a game and the final horn, that is what defined him. He used all the criticism and challenges as fuel to drive him to work harder and be better. He studied the game's history, his opponents' habits, and educated himself on even the tendencies of each official so he could dictate the outcome. Just as the Pistons had to overcome the challenge during that era of the Boston Celtics, the Chicago Bulls had to overcome the challenges of the Detroit Pistons. And Michael Jordan's efforts spread to others around him. They picked up his habits of wanting to be better to prove the naysayers wrong. Each challenge was taken on because he realized his limitations were in the amount of education he had in regard to every aspect of the game and worked to make them his strengths by becoming more educated than his opponents.

We all have the ability to fulfill every one of our goals in life. To do so, we simply have to accept the internal challenge. Whatever work is required for us to successfully accomplish our goals, we have to put forth that effort every day. When we reach one goal, we can then focus on the next. Each challenge is greater than the last challenge. We have to be willing to confront every challenge in front of us and do what is necessary to overcome them.

A great driver didn't one day start driving great. That person learned to drive and developed the skills to get better over time. That person made safety a part of their everyday ritual. He or she then followed all the same techniques continually until they became second nature. That's what we are learning to do with our mind. We are learning to create habits mentally that become a part of our everyday lives. What seems difficult for someone else will then become natural for you. Once it is natural, every time you create a new goal, you will be able to attain it because you will then possess the skills necessary to accomplish it easily. You will always find yourself assessing the situation before you delve into it. Rational thought always stands above irrational actions. If you have a rational thought, it is not possible to have an irrational action, because you would have thought the process out first.

In the end, when we are honest with ourselves about what we want to accomplish and reasonable in coming up with those ideals, we will be able to put in motion all the steps necessary to successfully complete that goal. It doesn't matter if it is in our personal or business life. Life is business as usual when you follow the same ideals you developed over time. You created a structured environment with a sound mental foundation. You develop an understanding that the reason for developing goals is for personal satisfaction, not because we want to impress others around us. You then grasp the understanding that in order to reach the ultimate victory, you must get through the small victories first.

In the end, we don't rest on what we've accomplished but instead look to expand the world we live in with new goals and dreams. We then work toward them, utilizing the skills we developed on the way to the goals that were completed in our past on an everyday basis, making each learned skill set look natural to others watching us until they become natural to us mentally.

With all you've done to this point in your development, you are ready for a new beginning. You have created a new person just by changing how you use your most valuable resource, your mind. You have established new boundaries for yourself by understanding that the life you live is yours and is lived for you. We have established the necessary building blocks to become that new person we desire to be. The elimination of negative voices has cleared our mind of the things that restricted us from taking on the challenges of new goals. Now every goal we have is attainable because we understand how to determine which goals require efforts that we control and are therefore reasonable. It is now time for a new beginning.

NEW BEGINNINGS

The ability to change how we view ourselves is an evolution of change that, over time, becomes a natural occurrence in life. We go from living a stagnant existence to living a life full of change and adventure. The fulfilling of dreams and the desire to be better today than we were yesterday becomes a part of us.

This is a new beginning in our lives. It is changing the nature and course of your life's direction to give you a better quality of life. You may not forget your past life, but when you reflect on it you will be able to smile at how strong you are and what you were able to accomplish. Your mental boundaries have been expanded, which has now allowed the entire world to be open to you.

We never stop learning. Our lives are ever changing, leaving us with only one desire, which is to complete the cycle of life and leave a positive legacy. When we reflect back on our lives, we want to be able to say, "Every goal I set for myself after my mental evolution, I completed to my satisfaction. In the end, I did it for me and I didn't let anyone discourage me from completing any tasks from that point, and you have to do it for you."

I don't have the ability to change what has already happened in my life, so I was able to focus solely on what was in front of me. I wouldn't allow myself to forget the past, because I had no desire to make the same mistakes, but I did move beyond them. Those things I may have done wrong or that may have affected other people's lives, I have forgiven myself for and moved forward.

What is important here is that we are able to see what we've done different in our lives to make us better than we ever thought we could be. Negative influences are now recognized for what they are. They are nothing more than words of inspiration from sources that don't know our inner strength. How inspiring is it to realize that every critical word told to you in your life was nothing more than a validation that you had the ability to accomplish great things or had moved beyond your past?

If life has taught us anything, it's that we cannot count on tomorrow to resolve the issues of today. Tomorrow is and always will be an excuse for not doing something today. You can't have a moment of completion without taking the necessary action with a task to reach the point of completion. We have to train ourselves to stop making excuses and respond to situations when they arise to ensure that they don't become a part of us and therefore become personal.

We're developing strategies that allow us to become a new person mentally. We are developing skills that are positive in our development and restructuring; becoming something that makes yesterday nothing more than an experience that allowed us to become the new person we are today. This is just the first step in development, but it sets the framework to developing and restructuring all aspects of our lives.

Education is the cornerstone for change. You can't change anything in your life without learning the lessons that brought about the desire to change. You were able to learn that something in your life wasn't working the way you desired and looked for an opportunity to change life's fortunes. That was your past education and applied as a foundation for change.

Anything new in life requires education. We are learning about different aspects of life and applying those items learned to our new mental structure. The development of the structure became possible because we were able to reinforce our foundation by considering the source of the materials used to establish that same foundation. If the source materials were poor, then we know that a solid reinforcement was necessary. That reinforcement could include, but is not limited to, the elimination of people in our lives who do not have a positive influence.

The new beginning is the same as starting over in life. Although you are aware of where you started, you know that in changing your way of viewing yourself that you are currently not in that place anymore. The understanding is that even with the changes and having moved to a different structural place in your life, you are still able to build on to what you have already established. This is simply the beginning of something bigger and better.

Every phase of mental development in our lives was a new beginning. Through education, we found multiple beginnings, and with the conclusion of each endeavor, we removed restrictions from our mental boundaries. In removing the lock on our mind that restricts unlimited growth, we have access to limitless goals and dreams. Imagine your life without mental restrictions in regard to your desires to do better things in your life.

The understanding is always that with enough education, our accomplishments can be to our individual satisfaction. Never should we do anything that requires us to look for others' approval to validate whether we have done something positive. It is positive if we feel that it was worthwhile and that what we learned in the end has opened up another avenue to our lives. The validation is in the ability to utilize what we have learned on a daily basis.

Life can be approached from one of two angles, and in choosing either angle, you will still end up with the same results. We can approach life as a business. We will utilize the strategies that make the business a success by following other successfully orchestrated business models. In doing so, we duplicate the ideals that brought someone else satisfactory results. It is important to educate ourselves on the things necessary to expand the boundaries that have limited what we have previously been unable to complete to our own satisfaction.

Life can also be orchestrated like a scientific experiment. Through the education of trial and error, we eliminate what has brought an unsatisfactory result until we find a solution that is to our satisfaction.

Where we stood yesterday is nothing more than a reflection of limitations that have been overcome today. We see how long a road we've traveled and are able to see how far we can travel tomorrow. With each mental destination, we are able to establish new boundaries and reinforce our foundation along the way. The limitless opportunities were made available because we were able to train our minds to understand that the positive can exist without the negative.

The understanding of relative terms has established our ability to prosper without fear. We have associated education with those relative terms and come to the understanding that relative gives the understanding that the term actually does not exist. We shall never forget that each term in itself applies to finality and does not apply to life due to the mind's ability to evolve and be educated until the final moment.

> "Failure" and "success" are relative terms in relation to life. Failure cannot exist in the presence of education. One cannot fail at anything if an education was obtained in the process. Success being the polar opposite, therefore, also cannot exist, as through education, the mind is ever evolving and thus never reaching the point of completion.

How beautiful is the thought that with each passing moment in time we are learning and evolving into something better than we were the moment before; that yesterday no longer exists and does not factor into today any more than today factors into tomorrow. We are *Trading Today for a Better Tomorrow*. It is an evolution in mental growth and development through education.

Now that we are learning to develop and implement the idealism that everything positive overrides everything negative, we now control all information associated with our mental development. We have now become our own source of inspiration and life has become our ongoing education. Today we can live because tomorrow can no longer exist.

www.ingramcontent.com/pod-product-compliance
Lightning Source LLC
LaVergne TN
LVHW020431080526
838202LV00055B/5126